ALL ABOARD FOR THE BOBO ROAD

Stephen Davies

Christopher Corr

ANDERSEN PRESS

At the Banfora bus station a crowd of chattering passengers are climbing aboard Big Ali's minibus.

"All aboard for the Bobo Road!" Big Ali booms.

"The most beautiful road in the world!"

High up on the roof of the minibus, helping to load the luggage, are Big Ali's children Fatima and Galo. Going to Bobo is a special treat and they are both very excited.

BEEP, BEEP – they're off!
The wheels
of the minibus
go round.

"Enjoy the ride!" Big Ali booms. "Next stop, Lake Tengréla."
Fatima and Galo are riding on the roof. They like looking after
the luggage and feeling the wind on their faces.

Beside the hippo lake, the bus slows down and stops.

There are people to board and luggage to load: two mopeds and three bicycles. Fatima and Galo use ropes to tie them down.

Beep, beep! They're off again.

"Goodbye, hippos!" Big Ali booms. "Next stop, Karfiguéla Falls."

Beside the waterfall, the bus slows down and stops.
There are more people to board and luggage to load:
four cans of cooking oil and five sacks of rice.

They're off again.

"Hold on tight," Big Ali booms. "Next stop, the Domes of Fabedougou."

In the shadow of the old rock domes,
the bus slows down and stops. There are
even more people to board and luggage to load:
six enormous yams and seven watermelons.
"Don't eat those melons, Galo!" says Fatima.
"They're not for you."

And then – BEEP, BEEP!
They're off again.
"I told you this road is beautiful,"
booms Big Ali. "Next stop, the magical
Forest of Mou."

In the middle of the deep, dark forest, the bus slows down and stops. This time the luggage is alive!

Eight ducks, nine goats and ten chickens. Fatima and Galo make the animals comfortable. And then – BEEP, BEEP! They're off again. "Next stop, Bobo!" booms Big Ali.

The minibus heads out of the forest and into a big city.
"Hooray!" shouts Fatima.
"We're here!"

They judder by fruit stalls and a caterpillar café,

past the train station and the Grand Mosque.

Finally they arrive at Bobo station.

"Everybody off!"

Wheezing and sneezing, Fatima and Galo
help Big Ali to unload ten chickens,
nine goats and eight ducks.
A donkey cart is waiting to take
the animals to market.

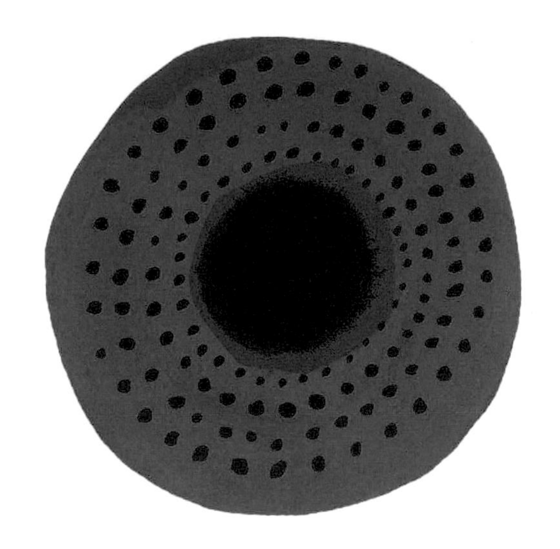

Huffing and puffing, Galo unloads
seven watermelons and six enormous yams.
Some women take the fruit and vegetables.
"Now we can set up our stall," they say.

Craning and straining, Fatima
unloads five sacks of rice and
four cans of cooking oil.

"Thank you," says a man.
"Now I can open
my restaurant."

Tired and hungry, the children help Big Ali to unload three bicycles and two mopeds.

“Thank you,” say their owners.
“See you again soon.”

All the luggage has been taken away, except for just one thing:
the big, round, mysterious package wrapped in cloth and string.
"Look!" says Fatima. "I wonder who that belongs to?"
"It belongs to you two," booms Big Ali. "You deserve it."
They open up the big, round package...

...and inside is a huge pot of rice, beans and fried fish!

Fatima and Gato wash their hands and sit down around the pot with their father.

"Another beautiful sight," breathes Bibi Ali, gazing at the sunset.

"Yes," say the children, gazing at the pot, "and it's delicious, too!"

LAKE TENGRÉLA
KARFIGUÉLA FALLS
BANFORA